Tiger Ways

To Claudia, George, Lisa and Mark – K.G.

To Mel, Jonathan and Jake – N.S.

TIGER WAYS
A RED FOX BOOK 978 0 099 48804 0

First published in Great Britain in 2007 by The Bodley Head,
an imprint of Random House Children's Publishers UK
A Random House Group Company

The Bodley Head edition published 2007
Red Fox edition published 2008

5 7 9 10 8 6 4

Text copyright © Kes Gray, 2007
Illustrations copyright © Nick Sharratt, 2007

Set in Lemonade

Red Fox Books are published by Random House Children's Publishers UK,
61-63 Uxbridge Road, London W5 5SA

www.daisyclub.co.uk

Addresses for companies within The Random House Group Limited can be found at:
www.randomhouse.co.uk/offices.htm

THE RANDOM HOUSE GROUP Limited Reg. No. 954009

A CIP catalogue record for this book is available from the British Library.

Printed in Singapore

Tiger Ways

Kes Gray & Nick Sharratt

RED FOX

Daisy had been adopted by tigers.

Her *mum* had been stolen by a gang of *mad* elephants,

so there was no one else around to look after her.

"Come with us," said the tiger chief, "and we
will teach you tiger ways."

"Excellent!" said Daisy, following the tigers
deep into the jungle.

"You'll have to grow a tail," said one of the tigers.

"No problem," said Daisy.

"And *you'll* need to get some stripes."

"I love stripes!" said Daisy, jumping over a small jungle stream.

"Where will I live?" asked Daisy.

"In a cave," said the tigers. "Caves are the tiger way."

"How exciting!" thought Daisy.

"Where will I sleep?" asked Daisy.

"On a ledge," said the tigers, "or up a tree.

That is the tiger way."

"How brilliant!" thought Daisy.

"And what will I eat?" Daisy asked.

"People, mostly," said the tigers. "People or antelopes –
it depends on what we can catch."

Daisy frowned. "People and antelopes?"

She'd never eaten those before!

She followed the tigers deeper into the jungle.

"You know when you're eating people and antelopes," Daisy asked, "do you have tomato sauce on them or do you eat them by themselves?"

"By themselves," said the tiger chief. "Tigers don't eat tomato sauce, it's not the tiger way. We eat everything on its own."

Daisy prowled through some jungle leaves and frowned again.
"I know what!" she said. "I've got a better idea. What if
sometimes we do things the tiger way, and other times we
do things *my way*! Then it will be much more fairer!"
"OK," said the tigers.

"So, like, if I'm eating people, I can have
tomato sauce on them," said Daisy.
"Fair enough," said the tigers.
"Or squirty cream," said Daisy.
"If you say so," said the tigers.

"Actually, thinking about it, it's probably better if I'm the tiger chief from now on," said Daisy.

"OK," said the tiger, who wasn't the tiger chief any more.

"One other thing," said Daisy. "I'll only eat people that I don't like. Like Jack Beechwhistle. I don't mind eating him because he calls everyone horrible names at school. Eating him would be all right . . . as long as he's got lots of tomato sauce on him."

The tigers nodded and led Daisy to their cave. Daisy grew a tail and some stripes and began learning tiger ways. She learned to clean her long tiger whiskers without soap, jump from really big boulders, hide in long grass and catch and eat people and antelopes.

"Tiger ways are fun!" roared Daisy.

The tigers learned to ride Daisy's bike, eat jelly beans, read comics, build sandcastles, watch telly, have cushion fights and bounce really high on trampolines.

"Daisy ways are fun too!"
whooped the tigers.

Daisy was just reaching for some more tomato sauce when her tiger ears pricked up. A dangerous sound was coming from high up in the jungle canopy.

"Daisy, will you come out from under the kitchen table," said the strange and dangerous sound. "It's time you went upstairs for a bath."

Daisy crouched low in the jungle grass.

Just her tiger luck. It was the sound of her mum.

The mad elephants must have given her back.

"Daisy, I know you're under there," said Mum. "You've been under there ever since we got back from the school fête. Will you please go and have your bath and wash that face paint off."

Daisy closed her eyes and
hid behind her big tiger paws.

"Daisy," growled her mum.

Daisy looked out from under the table and sighed.
"Oh, Mum, I can't have a bath. I'm a tiger," she said.
"Tigers are cats and cats don't like water. In fact,
they hate water. Baths aren't the tiger way."

Daisy's *mum* folded her arms. "Actually, Daisy, tigers do like water. In fact, tigers are very good swimmers!" "Not me," said Daisy. "I was frightened by a crocodile when I was a cub."

Daisy's *mum* raised her eyebrows and then smiled. "I know a tiger way!" she said.

"Hot milk!" said Daisy's mum. "Tigers love hot milk. How about if you have your bath and get ready for bed, and I make you a tiger-sized cup of hot milk!"

Daisy did a tiger tut and
crawled out of her tiger cave.
"Okayyyyyy," she sighed.
"But you're going to have
to help me brush my
teeth tonight."

"And why would that be,
Little Miss Tiger?"
asked Daisy's mum.

"Because I ate Jack Beechwhistle for lunch earlier," purred Daisy.

"And I've still got some bits of him stuck between my teeth!

Raaaaaahhhhhhh!!!"

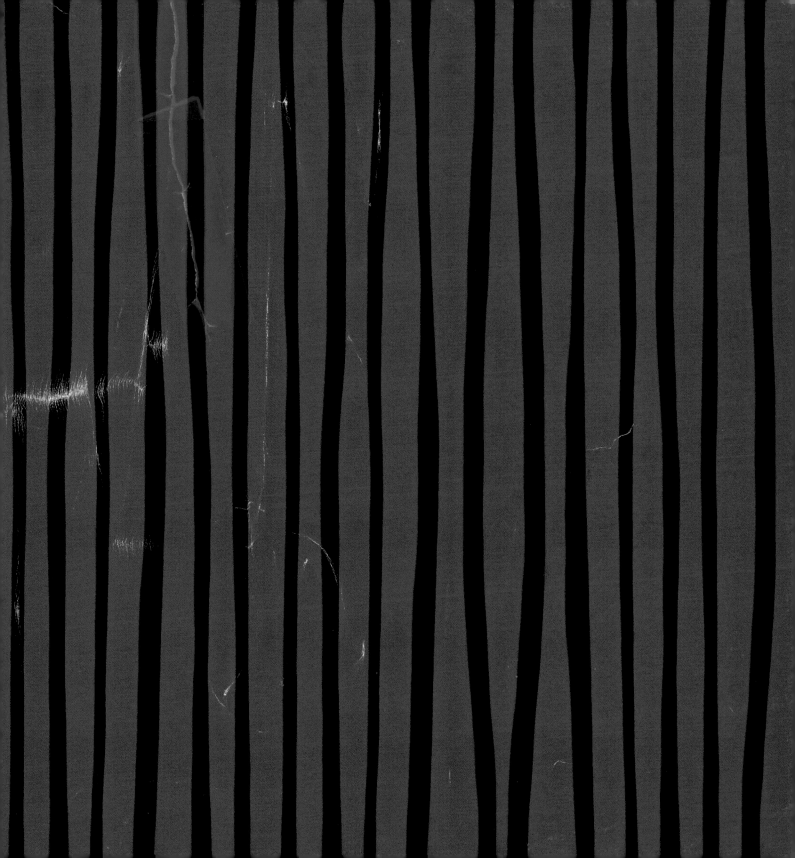

Find out more about Daisy!

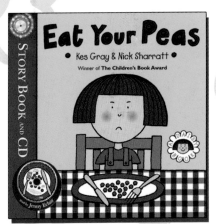

New longer Daisy story books!

Come and play with Daisy at www.daisyclub.co.uk